The Boxcar Children Mysteries

THE MYSTERY OF THE
STAR RUBY

created by
GERTRUDE CHANDLER WARNER

Illustrated by Hodges Soileau

SCHOLASTIC INC.
New York Toronto London Auckland Sydney
New Delhi Mexico City Hong Kong Buenos Aires

ISBN 0-439-35372-6

12 11 10 9 8 7 6 5 4   7/0

Printed in the U.S.A.   40
First Scholastic printing, July 2002

Contents

CHAPTER 1

The Contest

"I wish we didn't have to go back to Greenfield," said six-year-old Benny Alden.

Violet turned from the front seat of the car. "Don't you miss our house?" she asked her little brother.

"And our boxcar?" put in Henry, sitting next to Benny.

Jessie, who was twelve, knew how Benny felt.

"The boxcar is important," she said. "It's where we lived before Grandfather found us. Benny just doesn't want this vacation to end."

"We did have a great time camping in the mountains," their grandfather, James Alden, agreed. "It seems a shame to leave the area so soon."

Benny became excited. "Does that mean we can stay longer?"

Grandfather smiled at him in the rear-view mirror.

"We'll see."

The Alden children looked at one another. They knew "we'll see" often meant "okay."

As they drove along the Blue Ridge Parkway, Henry spotted a sign.

" 'Ruby Hollow Gem Mine and Resort,' " he read aloud. " 'Rock Hounds Welcome.' "

"A gem mine!" ten-year-old Violet exclaimed. "That sounds great! Can we go there?"

"It does sound interesting," said Grandfather. "We'll check it out."

"Oh, boy!" Benny bounced in his seat.

Then he asked, "What's a rock hound? Is it a dog made of rocks?"

Henry laughed. "A rock hound is someone who collects rocks and minerals." At fourteen, Henry was used to answering Benny's questions.

They turned off the main highway, following signs that led them from one twisting road to another. Jessie worried they would never find the gem mine — or their way out again!

At last the thick woods parted to reveal a clearing. A large sign with a giant painted red jewel proclaimed they had arrived at Ruby Hollow.

Grandfather followed the driveway into a crowded parking lot. They got out of the car and walked up a flower-lined path to a series of wooden buildings. At the main building, a man in a cowboy hat opened the entrance door and waved them inside.

"Come in," he said. "I'm Cecil Knight, the owner of Ruby Hollow. I hope you plan to stay because we have lots to do here. Besides the mine, we have hiking trails, a restaurant, a museum, and a gem-cutting shop. I've got two cabins and a room left in the main building."

"I didn't realize so many people would be here," said James Alden.

Cecil Knight tapped a poster on the wall in the lobby. "They come for the annual gem contest. It lasts a week. The person who finds the largest ruby by the end of the week wins first place. You're just in time to take part!"

The children were looking at the framed photographs and newspaper clippings that hung on the wall. The pictures showed people holding red or blue stones. Some of the stones were pretty big.

"What do you win in the contest?" asked Henry.

"First place is a cash prize of one thousand dollars," Mr. Knight replied. "Winners get their picture in the local paper. And our on-site jeweler will set the stone in the mounting of their choice. Solid gold, of course."

Benny pointed to a photograph of a boy holding what looked like a big blue marble.

"Violet, will you take a picture of me with my marbles?" he said.

Mr. Knight chuckled. "That's not a marble, son. The boy in that photo was twelve years old. He found a 1,497-carat sapphire worth eleven thousand dollars."

The children gasped.

"Grandfather, can we stay?" Benny asked eagerly. He wanted to start digging for gems right away.

"I guess we'll need those cabins and that room," Grandfather told Mr. Knight. "The children will take the cabins. I'll stay in the main building."

"Come back to my office." Mr. Knight led the way down a short hall.

Knotty-pine paneled walls were crowded with more photographs. But these pictures were older, in black and white instead of color.

While Grandfather registered, Benny studied a photo of two boys standing by a big wooden wheel. One boy grinned into the camera, but the other slouched with his hands in his pockets, frowning.

Once they were checked in, Mr. Knight explained some of the procedures.

"There's a five-dollar entry fee for each person, every day you work on the flume line," he said. "Buckets range in price from five dollars each up to fifty dollars for a family-sized bucket. All our specialty buckets are guaranteed to produce gemstones."

Violet didn't understand. "Don't we go dig in the mine?"

"Ruby Hollow Mine closed fifty years ago," Mr. Knight told her. "What we do is bulldoze ore from the creek and around the mine. There are plenty of stones in this region! If you look carefully, you can actually find rubies along the roads."

"Wow!" said Benny. "Let's go!"

"When you're ready, go down to the flume," said Cecil Knight. "Someone down there will get you started."

"Let's settle in first," Grandfather said, taking the keys Mr. Knight handed him.

As they walked back to the car, Grandfather pointed out the two empty cabins. "There's Garnet. And the one two doors down is Mica."

"What funny names for cabins," commented Jessie.

"A garnet is a semiprecious gem," said Henry, reading from a brochure. "And mica is a mineral. Why don't Benny and I take Mica, and you girls can stay in Garnet."

After retrieving their luggage from the trunk, the children went to their cabins.

Benny liked the one he was sharing with Henry. It had pine bunk beds and old-fashioned mining lamps hanging on the walls.

"Top bunk is mine!" he claimed.

"Okay," said Henry. "I hope the girls aren't unpacking. I want to start looking for rubies."

The girls did, too. They were waiting outside the boys' cabin.

"Here comes Grandfather," said Jessie. "Can we hunt for rubies now?"

James Alden glanced at the sun sinking

behind the pines. "Well, it's pretty late. But I'm just as eager as you are. Let's go!"

They walked down a trail marked FLUME. At the end was a booth. Grandfather paid the entry fees to the girl inside.

"You get a complimentary bucket your first day," she said, handing over a large bucket filled with dirt. "Good luck!"

The flume was directly ahead of them. A waterwheel turned wooden paddles, supplying a steady stream of fresh creek water that flowed through a long, V-shaped wooden trough. People lined both sides of the trough, sifting dirt in mesh-screened trays.

Near one end of the flume was a stack of mesh-bottomed trays.

Grandfather scanned the brochure. "We each take one of these trays. Then we'll go work on the flume."

"What's a flume?" asked Benny.

"That long wooden thing with water going through it," answered Grandfather. "The waterwheel keeps the water moving so you can rinse the dirt."

Benny recognized the waterwheel as the

wooden wheel in the photograph in Mr. Knight's office.

The Aldens found places along the flume. People shifted to make room for them.

A young man with sandy hair and glasses smiled at Benny.

"Your first try at panning?" he asked.

Benny nodded, holding up his tray. "I want to find the biggest ruby in the world."

The young man laughed. "Don't we all. My name is Jonathan Merrill. I've been coming to Ruby Hollow every summer since I was in high school. I'm nearly out of college now, but I still like to come here."

Grandfather introduced himself. "These are my grandchildren — Henry, Jessie, Violet, and Benny. I'm afraid we're all beginners."

"It's a lot of fun," said Jonathan. "I'll give you some pointers. First, don't put too much ore on your tray." He scooped some dirt from the bucket and dumped it onto each tray.

Benny wrinkled his nose. "How am I going to find a ruby in that mess?"

"Here comes the fun part," Jonathan told him. "Dip your tray into the water, then rinse. See? Some of the mud washes down the flume."

"But my tray is still muddy," said Jessie.

"You have to keep rinsing," Jonathan instructed. "Rinse and then shift the rocks around. You have to do this until the water runs clear. Then you'll be able to see the rocks that are left."

The Aldens rinsed and tilted their trays, letting the muddy dirt wash away.

"Is this good enough?" Benny asked Jonathan.

"Not yet. Keep rinsing."

After a while, Jonathan checked their trays. "Great! Now let's see what you've got." He sorted through the small stones in Violet's tray first.

"I don't see any rubies," she said. "All I see are a bunch of rocks."

"Rubies and sapphires don't come out of the ground polished and cut like you see in jewelry stores," Jonathan said. "They're embedded in matrix, a rocky material. So they look like rocks at first."

Jessie peered into her own tray. "If they look like rocks, how will we ever know we found a ruby?"

"There are clues to help you identify gems in the rough," said Jonathan. "Visit the Ruby Hollow Gem Museum. There are displays to help you see what rubies and other gems look like with and without matrix."

"I can see there's more to this than we thought," Grandfather said with a laugh.

"You'll catch on fast." Jonathan leaned over Grandfather's tray and sorted swiftly through the stones. He held up a black rock. "This is obsidian."

"What do I have?" Benny asked.

Jonathan examined the stones in Benny's tray. He dropped a tiny stone into Benny's palm.

"Here's a sapphire," he said. "Nice going!"

"A sapphire!" Benny cried.

Jessie's and Violet's trays contained pretty chunks of pink quartz. Henry's tray yielded a nice-sized garnet.

"Not bad for your first day," Jonathan pronounced.

Benny put his sapphire in his pocket. "Rock-hunting makes me hungry!"

Grandfather laughed. "Everything makes you hungry. But it *is* dinnertime."

"I'll walk with you up to the restaurant," said Jonathan. They all turned in their trays and washed up at the old-fashioned outdoor pump.

The restaurant was inside the main building. Outside the entrance, the menu was written on a chalkboard. Guests dined family-style at the big pine tables.

Jonathan and the Aldens sat down.

They were soon joined by a woman around Grandfather's age and a dark-haired man wearing sunglasses and a white cotton shirt.

"I'm Sybil Finley," the elderly woman at the table said. She wore a white oversized man's shirt and carried a straw hat. "I saw Jonathan helping you on the flume."

"Is this your first day, too?" Benny wanted to know. He popped a hush puppy in his mouth, enjoying the crunchy sweetness of fried cornmeal and onion.

Sybil grinned at him. "Not hardly. I've been a rock hound my whole life. I've been to every gem mine around. But I keep coming back to Ruby Hollow."

"What brings you back?" Grandfather asked.

"Well, it's the only mine that has star rubies," replied Sybil. "And I also enjoy the contest."

"You might as well go home, Sybil," the dark-haired man spoke up, pulling off his sunglasses. "*I'm* going to win that contest."

CHAPTER 2

Mysterious Lights

"How come you're going to win?" Benny asked the man, who'd said his name was Donald Hodge. "The contest doesn't end till Saturday."

"Because I found a Papa Bear ruby," Donald said smugly. "It'll be a challenge for anyone to find a bigger stone."

He pulled a black velvet bag from his pocket and opened the drawstring. A large pinkish rock with red glints tumbled onto his place mat.

Jonathan whistled. "Is that the stone you found in your last bucket today?"

As Jonathan reached for the rock, Donald deftly scooped it up and dropped it back into the velvet bag. "Can't touch my contest winner," he said jokingly.

"Like Benny said, the week's not over," Sybil reminded Donald. "Somebody could find a ruby in that class that's bigger than yours, you know."

Cecil Knight came around with the coffeepot. "Coffee, anyone?" he asked.

"I drink tea," said Sybil. "But you know that, Cecil."

"I'll send the waitress over with hot water," Mr. Knight said. "Coffee, Mr. Hodge?"

"Thanks," said Donald. His napkin fell to the floor.

Henry bent down to pick it up, but Donald planted his foot on the red-checked cloth.

"I've got it," he whispered hoarsely, bending down under the table.

While Mr. Knight poured coffee into his

cup, Donald took a long time to retrieve his napkin.

Weird, thought Henry.

"How did you all do on your first day?" Mr. Knight asked Grandfather.

"I found a sapphire!" Benny exclaimed, pulling the small stone from his pocket.

"Way to go!" said Mr. Knight. "A perfect Baby Bear."

Benny stared at his stone. "I thought it was a rock."

Mr. Knight laughed. "It is a rock, Benny. Let me explain the Ruby Hollow grading system. I use the Three Bears story to make it easy to remember. Any gem under fifteen carats is called a Baby Bear. A Mama Bear gem is fifteen to thirty carats, worth cutting for jewelry. And a Papa Bear is any gem over thirty carats."

"I didn't know bears ate carrots," said Benny, making them all laugh.

"We're not talking about the vegetable," said Donald. "A carat is the unit used to measure gems. Just like your weight is measured in pounds."

"Good luck tomorrow. Give Mr. Hodge some competition," Mr. Knight said, moving on to the next table.

Violet had been thinking about the Three Bears story.

"What about Goldilocks? Is there a Goldilocks size of ruby?"

"There *is* a Goldilocks category," said Jonathan. "It's not a size, though, but a special kind of ruby. It's called a star ruby."

"What's so special about a star ruby?" Jessie wanted to know.

"Regular rubies look like this." Sybil leaned forward and held out her hand. A brilliant red stone glittered in a ring on her left hand. "But a star ruby has six rays, like the rays of the sun."

Jonathan pointed to Sybil's ring. "See how the stone is cut so it catches the light? That's called faceting. A star ruby is polished smooth so you can see the rays inside."

"Has anybody ever found a star ruby here?" asked Henry.

"Only a few people," Jonathan answered.

"Ruby Hollow is the only mine in these mountains where you can find star rubies. I've been coming here for years and I've never found one."

"Neither have I," added Sybil. "A star ruby is the only stone I don't have in my collection. I'd do *anything* to find one." She gave a big sigh.

"I'd love to pick up such an unusual gem, too," said Jonathan. "For my fiancée's engagement ring."

"Maybe we'll all be lucky this week," said Henry.

"Mmmmm," said Benny, waiting for Jessie to ladle gravy on his potatoes. "This is like eating at home."

Grandfather passed around the platter of chicken. "I like the homey atmosphere, too."

"That's because it's a family-run mine," said Sybil. "Cecil's family bought the mine about fifty years ago. I think the family had a falling-out sometime after that. Cecil's uncle thought the mine should be his. But Cecil has been running this mine ever since I can remember."

"Imagine owning a ruby mine!" Jessie said. "Wouldn't that be neat?"

"Cecil has worked hard to make this place a success," Sybil said. "I hope he can hang on to the mine and do well. He deserves it."

Just then the waitress returned with plates of peach cobbler topped with melting vanilla ice cream.

At the same moment, Donald rose from his chair so abruptly he collided with her.

Henry jumped up in time to save the tray from crashing to the floor.

"I'm sorry!" Donald said to the waitress. "I didn't see you."

"It's okay," she said. "This young man saved the dessert!"

"Excuse me," Donald said to the others at the table. "I'm not a big fan of peach cobbler." He left the dining room.

"*I'm* a big fan of peach cobber," Benny said to the waitress. "You can give me his, too."

Everyone laughed.

Jessie was still thinking about the contest.

"How can Mr. Knight afford to pay the prize money if his business isn't doing so well?"

"A lot of people come here for the contest," Sybil said. "They pay for entry fees, lodging, and meals in the restaurant, have their stones mounted in jewelry, and buy buckets of pre-spaded dirt."

"Serious rock hounds don't buy the five-dollar buckets," Jonathan added. "They spring for the more expensive specialty buckets."

After dinner, the grown-ups lingered in the rocking chairs on the wide front porch.

The Alden kids strolled down one of the trails behind the cabins. Crickets chirped their end-of-summer song. The mountains rose darkly around them. No moon or stars could be seen in the pitch-black sky.

"Boy," murmured Henry. "When it's night here, it's really night!"

"I can't wait to start looking for rubies tomorrow," said Jessie.

"Me, too," Benny agreed. "Maybe one of *us* will win the contest."

"We'd have to find a Papa Bear ruby bigger than Mr. Hodge's," said Violet.

"We have as good a chance as anyone else here," Jessie said confidently.

Snap! Cra-ack!

Henry spun around. "What was that?"

"It sounded like a twig breaking," Violet said, her heart pounding. What would be in the woods after dark? A bear? A fox?

Suddenly Benny cried, "Look!"

Everyone looked up at the sky. It wasn't pitch-black anymore.

A round, reddish light like a globe appeared over the peak of a distant mountain. The light hovered in the air a few seconds, then vanished. A moment later, the light reappeared, but in a different spot. Then it was gone again.

"Wow!" exclaimed Henry. "What was *that*?"

Benny's voice was low. "It could only be one thing."

"What?" chorused Jessie and Violet.

"A flying saucer," he replied solemnly.

CHAPTER 3

Jewels in the Dirt

"Benny, there are no flying saucers," Jessie said.

"What else can it be?" he insisted.

The children watched for a few more minutes. But the reddish round light did not reappear.

"We'd better get back," Henry said. "It's pretty late."

They walked to the cabins. Lamplight shone through the window of the cabin next to Garnet, the girls' cabin.

Jessie glanced up at the sky once more.

No strange light. She knew it wasn't a flying saucer. But what else could it have been?

Loud caws in the pine trees woke Jessie the next morning.

"Those crows are a good alarm clock," she told Violet as they got dressed. "Who could sleep through that racket?"

The boys were waiting for them outside their cabin. The door to the cabin next to Violet's and Jessie's opened and Sybil Finley stepped out. Her cabin was called Sapphire.

"Good morning," she greeted them. "I didn't know you girls were in Garnet. We're neighbors!"

They all walked to the restaurant. The day's forecast — hot and sunny — was printed on the chalkboard, along with the breakfast specials, "Gold Nuggets and Potato Pebbles."

Jonathan was sitting at their table, scribbling in a notebook.

"I saw an eastern kingbird on my morning walk," he said. "I've never seen one before. I'm adding it to my bird list."

"You keep a bird list?" Violet asked.

"I keep lists for everything," Jonathan said, holding up a small black notebook. "I write down the mileage on my car, the weather, even what I eat for breakfast."

"I should start a food list," Benny said.

Henry laughed. "You'd need a pretty big notebook just for one day!"

Grandfather and Donald Hodge joined them. Donald wore a white button-down shirt. Violet thought it was strange he was so dressed up to hunt for rubies.

"Grandfather!" Benny exclaimed. "We saw a flying saucer last night!"

"A flying saucer in North Carolina!" Sybil laughed.

"We did see strange lights over the mountain," Henry said. "They were round and kind of red."

"You don't really believe in that stuff, do you?" Donald scoffed. When he picked up his cup, he spilled coffee on the front of his shirt.

"You should dab water on that," Jessie advised. "Coffee stains are hard to get out."

"It's okay," Donald said. "There's a Laundromat here." He looked up just as Cecil came over. "In fact," Donald said, "I'd better go there now." He hurried away.

"Did you kids see the Brown Mountain Lights last night?" Cecil asked.

"Is that what they're called?" asked Henry. "What causes them?"

"No one knows for sure, but scientists believe the lights are formed from a combination of gases in the rocks in Brown Mountain. People have seen those lights over the mountain for a hundred years," Cecil said.

"I didn't see any lights last night," Sybil said. "Did you, Jonathan?"

"No, I was working on my lists last night," he said.

"Not everybody is lucky enough to see them," said Cecil. "But they are more common this time of year on moonless nights."

Their waitress arrived with breakfast — "Gold Nugget" scrambled eggs, "Potato Pebble" fries, ham, and juice.

Benny ate quickly. The mysterious lights were neat, but the idea of finding a Papa

Bear ruby was even more exciting. He couldn't wait to start!

After breakfast, the children changed into old clothes and shoes and shouldered their backpacks. They met Grandfather in the Ruby Hollow Gem Museum.

The glass cases displayed hundreds of gems and minerals.

"I never knew there were so many different rocks." Henry read the names aloud. "Hiddenite, epodite, obsidian, blue calcite, emerald, sapphire, garnet, quartz — "

"Look at this." Jessie pointed to a showcase of rubies. "This is how rubies look when they come out of the ground, with rock around them. And these rubies over here are cut out of the rock."

Brilliant red stones lay on white velvet, some faceted to catch the sun, some polished smooth as glass. One sparkling gem caught Violet's eye.

"A star ruby!" she exclaimed. "See the six rays? It does look like a star."

Benny was eager to find his own rubies. "Can we go now?" he asked.

"Let's hit the flume line!" Grandfather agreed.

Outside, they took the path to the flume. Grandfather paid their entry fees and bought them each a five-dollar bucket and plastic containers for their findings.

Jonathan and Sybil were already working on the flume. The kids found places between them.

A few minutes later, Donald Hodge came down the path, pushing a wheelbarrow with six buckets. He squeezed between Grandfather and Violet, making everyone on the line adjust.

Violet wondered why he just didn't go to the end of the line. She noticed the dirt in his buckets was finer and darker than hers.

"Your dirt looks different from mine," she remarked.

"I got enriched ore," Donald said. "I don't like messing with those native stone buckets. Mine are guaranteed to have some gems."

"Enriched buckets are also called 'salted,' " Jonathan explained. "That means each bucket definitely has gems in it. They could have been spaded from any mine. The dirt is looser and easier to rinse. But native buckets only come from Ruby Hollow. The ore hasn't been disturbed for thousands of years. That's why we have to rinse so much."

"Some of the finest gems can be found in the native mine," Sybil added. "But the buckets aren't guaranteed. That's what makes it fun — you never know what you're going to find!"

Benny had finished rinsing. He began sorting through his stones.

"Is this a ruby?" he asked Jonathan, holding up a tiny pinkish stone.

"Definitely. Put it in your plastic box so you don't lose it."

"Oh, boy! I found a ruby!" Benny dumped more dirt into his tray and began rinsing.

Jessie watched how fast Jonathan and Sybil worked, rinsing, sorting, and selecting stones before emptying the rest of the tray into the dumping pile behind the flume.

Donald Hodge worked even faster, but he dumped half a bucket of dirt into his tray at a time and didn't rinse properly.

"All I've found are a couple of puny sapphires!" he grumbled. "Cecil Knight ripped me off!"

"Cecil is as honest as the day is long," Sybil said loyally. "Maybe you should put a little less dirt into your tray."

"I don't have all day," Donald said. "And it's hot out here."

It *was* hot. Although the flume was shaded, panning was hot work.

Finally, Donald threw his empty buckets into the wheelbarrow and left, disgusted that he hadn't found a big stone.

Jessie watched him leave. *Boy, he really takes mining seriously*, she thought.

"I guess Donald expects to find a Papa Bear ruby every day," Sybil said. She eyed the dumping pile behind Donald's place on the flume. "I bet there are good stones in his dirt that he missed."

Jonathan ruefully shook his plastic container. "I only found three Baby Bear rubies and a sapphire. Not even worth taking to the grading window."

After three hours, the Aldens had finished going through their buckets. Everyone trooped to the grading window at the jewelry shop to have their stones weighed and inspected. Several people fell in line behind them, including Sybil Finley.

"Let's see what you have," the man at the counter told Benny, taking Benny's plastic container. "Not bad — two Baby Bear rubies. Pretty good for a beginner."

Grandfather had some nice hiddenite. Henry and Jessie each had a couple of small sapphires and garnets.

When it was Violet's turn, she handed her plastic container across the counter.

"I only found one," she said. "I don't think I'm a very good rock-finder."

The gem inspector peered at her stone through a special lens on his glasses.

Then he smiled at Violet.

"You're a better rock-finder than you think!" he said.

CHAPTER 4

The Mixed-up Backpacks

"What did I find?" Violet asked anxiously.

The man at the grading counter held up her stone between his thumb and forefinger.

"A very nice Mama Bear ruby," he proclaimed. "I'd say it's easily twenty carats."

"Wow!" exclaimed Benny.

The gem inspector put the stone in the plastic container and returned it to Violet. "Congratulations, young lady. Let me know if you decide to have the stone cut and mounted in a ring."

"I will. Thanks." Violet slipped the plastic container into her pink backpack. As she headed for the door, she noticed Sybil Finley standing in line behind her.

Sybil stared at Violet's backpack with a frown. Then, without speaking to Violet or the other Aldens, she pushed her way out of the jewelry shop and headed toward the cabins.

"What's with her?" Henry wondered.

Jessie shrugged, adjusting her own backpack. "Maybe she remembered she had to do something in her cabin. The line back there was pretty long."

"Is it time for lunch yet?" Grandfather asked.

Benny stopped in surprise. "Grandfather! That's what I always say!"

"Just thought I'd beat you to it!" said Grandfather.

Everyone laughed as they walked up the path to the main building.

Jonathan and Donald Hodge were sitting at their table in the dining room.

"I hear you had a pretty productive morning," Jonathan said to Violet. "May I see the stone you found?"

Violet slipped her backpack off and hooked it on the back of her chair. Then she unzipped the outside pocket and handed Jonathan the plastic container.

Jonathan gave a low whistle of admiration. "This would make a nice ring." He showed the stone to Donald. "See? If you'd stayed on the line longer, you might have found something."

"Beginner's luck," Donald said. "But it is a nice stone."

Jonathan passed the container back to Violet. "Donald has such a good eye, he never takes his stones to the grading window."

Donald flagged down their waitress. "Miss? When is lunch?"

"Coming right out, sir," she said.

Henry wondered why Donald was always bugging the waitress. Everyone was hungry, but they'd learned to wait, since meals were served family-style. Why was he so impatient?

Sybil Finley hurried into the dining

room. She had changed into a white blouse and denim skirt. When she saw an empty chair next to Violet, she smiled.

"I thought I was late," she said. She pulled out the empty chair, bumping Violet's bulky backpack.

"Let me move that," said Violet.

"I'll just put it over here." Sybil shifted the backpack to the floor, on the side away from Violet.

After a lunch of barbecue sandwiches, potato chips, pickles, and brownies, the Alden kids decided to spend the afternoon hiking.

"May I have my backpack?" Violet asked Sybil.

"I'm sorry, I forgot all about it." Sybil handed over the pink backpack. "Have fun."

The kids took a trail on the other side of the flume. The path followed the stream that fueled the waterwheel. The sun blazed overhead, but a breeze stirred the treetops.

"That water looks really good," Benny murmured. "Can we go wading?"

"Great idea," Henry said, unhooking the straps of his pack.

The Aldens sat down on the rocks and took off their shoes and socks. Leaving packs and water bottles on a big rock, they stepped out on a sandbar.

Jessie dipped her toes into the clear water, then yanked her foot back with a shriek. "Oooo, that's cold!"

Giggling, the kids waded into the chilly, shallow water. Olive-green minnows darted around their ankles as they picked up interesting stones.

Cra-ack! Crack!

Henry straightened up. "What was that?"

Violet pointed into the woods on the far side of the creek. "It sounded like it came from over there."

"Let's check it out," said Benny, already halfway across the stream.

On the opposite side, the kids clambered up the bank. They stared into the thick woods.

"We can't investigate without our shoes," Jessie said sensibly.

Henry shielded his eyes from the sun. "I don't see anything anyway. It was probably an animal."

"It must have been a *big* animal," Benny commented.

"Not necessarily," said Henry. "Everything is louder in the woods. I've heard chipmunks that sound like bears!"

They recrossed the stream. On the other side, they put on their shoes and socks, then sorted out their packs.

"Wait a minute!" Jessie exclaimed. "My pack is gone!"

Violet sat back on her heels. "You're right! What could have happened to it?"

"That cracking sound we heard must have been a person," Henry figured. "And he — or she — took Jessie's pack. But why?"

"Let's look around for clues," Violet suggested.

Benny found something right away, a scrap of white cloth caught on a tree branch.

Jessie plucked the material off the branch. "Good job, Benny. This could have been

here all along — but maybe not." She examined the fabric. "The cloth is stained."

"So all we have to do is find a ripped shirt or blouse with a stain on it," said Henry. "And that could belong to the person who took Jessie's pack."

Jessie gave her brother a dubious look. "Sounds like we're looking for a needle in a haystack!"

That evening at dinner, a thunderstorm broke over the mountains. Everyone marveled at the echoing thunder and bold streaks of lightning.

Looking at the rain pelting against the windows, Jonathan said ruefully, "And I changed my shirt before dinner."

The Aldens glanced at one another.

Henry whispered to Violet, "I wonder if Jonathan changed out of a ripped, stained, white shirt?"

Violet frowned. She didn't like to think of Jonathan doing something so dishonest.

Dinner arrived and soon everyone was busy eating turkey with dressing and mashed potatoes. While the waitress served slices of coconut cake, Cecil Knight filled coffee cups.

Jonathan turned to Benny. "Do you know where horses go when they are sick?"

Benny thought hard. "No. Where?"

"The horse-pital!"

Benny collapsed with laughter. "That's funny! Tell another one!"

"Okay, what do gorillas eat for lunch?"

"Bananas?" Benny guessed.

"Go-rilla cheese sandwiches!" Jonathan said.

Benny giggled. "I get it!"

At the front of the room, Mr. Knight clapped his hands. "Who wants to play charades?"

"What kind of a game is that?" Benny asked.

"You know, Benny. It's where you act out a word or a name and other people guess what it is," Jessie replied.

"My aunt Cathy was great at charades," said Mr. Knight. "I didn't know her very well — she and my uncle Josh and my cousin only visited the mine once when I was a kid. But I liked her a lot."

"Count me out," said Donald. "I've got a good book to read." He stood up to leave.

"It's still raining," said Violet. "You'll get wet."

"I won't melt." Donald disappeared into the stormy night.

"Well, I'm a charade-player from way back," said Sybil. "Let's pick a theme. How about animals?"

They all had fun guessing which animal each player acted out. When it finally stopped raining, it was time for bed.

Since it was dark outside, Henry and Benny walked the girls to their cabin.

Violet spotted something pink lying against the door.

"Jessie!" she cried. "It's your pack!"

Jessie picked up her pack.

"It's not even wet!" she exclaimed in amazement. "How did it get here?" Quickly, she unzipped the compartments. "Nothing is missing."

"That's weird," Henry said. "Why would

someone take your pack in the first place?"

"It's a mystery!" Benny said eagerly.

"It *is* strange," agreed Henry. "The Case of the Disappearing and Returning Backpack. But now, we'd better turn in. We have another day of hunting rubies tomorrow."

Later, after she and Jessie were in bed, Violet wondered about Jessie's missing backpack. Who could have taken it? What had the thief been after?

Then she thought of something. She sat up and switched on the lamp.

"What is it?" Jessie asked sleepily.

"I just realized something," said Violet. "Your pack looks just like mine! They are identical."

Now Jessie sat up. "Do you think the thief got our packs mixed up? That he took mine by mistake?"

"I don't know," Violet said. "But I think Benny's right. We definitely have a mystery here!"

CHAPTER 5

The Figure in White

The next morning, the kids met outside Violet and Jessie's cabin to discuss the mystery.

"My backpack is the same as Jessie's," Violet said. "Suppose the person took Jessie's *accidentally*?"

Henry nodded. "That makes sense. The person could have been after yours. What was in your backpack that wasn't in Jessie's?"

"The ruby!" Benny said instantly.

Violet's eyes widened. "They must have

been after the Mama Bear ruby I found. But why? It's not that big — Donald Hodge has a Papa Bear ruby that's much bigger than mine."

"We don't know *why* yet," said Jessie. "But we might be able to figure out *who*. Let's look for footprints."

Although the ground around the girls' cabin was muddy, it had rained again early that morning. If there had been footprints, they had washed away.

"Oh, well," Henry said practically. "We've never solved a mystery before breakfast."

The kids found Grandfather in the lobby of the main building, talking to Donald. They all went into the dining room.

Jonathan and Sybil were already seated and had the local newspaper spread out on their table.

"What's in the news?" Grandfather asked, sitting down.

"Last night's storm did a lot of damage to the town near here," Jonathan replied. "High winds blew a tree over on the public library."

Henry was reading over Jonathan's shoulder. "The tree hit the roof of the children's room. The rain soaked all the books."

"That's terrible," said Jessie, who loved to read. If the books in the library back home in Greenfield were ruined, she would feel awful.

Everyone discussed the storm over a breakfast of French toast, sausage, and scrambled eggs.

Rolling up the sleeves of her men's work shirt, Sybil declared, "It's going to be hot today. We'd better hit the flume early."

"How about if we go creekin', instead?" Jonathan suggested.

"What's that?" Benny asked.

"Instead of buying buckets of pre-spaded dirt, you can dig at a special place right in the stream," Jonathan explained. "It's fun. Want to come?"

"Yeah!" the Alden kids chorused.

"I think I'll stay on the flume line," Grandfather decided.

"Me, too," said Donald. "I stand a better chance of finding good stones by panning.

Though so far nobody has challenged my Papa Bear ruby. If no one does, I'll be driving that new convertible sports car, after all."

"You're selling your ruby to buy a sports car?" asked Henry.

Donald nodded.

"The contest prize money will be the down payment." He stood, jamming his hands in his pockets. "Coming, Sybil?"

"I believe I'll go with Jonathan and the kids," said Sybil. "Maybe I'll find a star ruby in the creek. It'll be cooler there, anyway."

After paying their entry fees, the Alden children, Sybil, and Jonathan took the trail down to the stream where digging was allowed.

Jonathan opened a small shed and brought out spades, buckets, and mesh trays.

Sybil put on her straw hat and waved her spade. "I'm going over there," she said. "Bet I find the biggest stone!"

"We'll go below those boulders," Jonathan told the Aldens. "Rubies and sapphires are heavy stones. They are more likely to collect behind big rocks than wash downstream."

They sat down on the grassy bank and removed their shoes and socks. Then, with squeals and shrieks, they waded into the rushing stream.

"This water is *cold*!" Jonathan exclaimed.

"We found that out yesterday," said Jessie. She almost added that when they went wading yesterday, someone stole her backpack.

But then she recalled the scrap of cloth. Suppose Jonathan had taken her pack. He *did* mention at dinner that he had changed his shirt.

"Don't dig big holes," Jonathan instructed. "Fill your buckets about half full, then rinse in the trays just like you do on the flume line. Remember, rubies and sapphires are dense and will settle in the bottom of your tray."

"Maybe one of us will find a star ruby," said Violet.

Jonathan nodded. "Maybe, Violet. You never know."

Cecil Knight came halfway down the trail. "I forgot to give you the key to the shed," he called to Jonathan.

"It's okay," Jonathan called back. "The shed was unlocked."

Henry wondered if Cecil Knight normally left the equipment shed unlocked overnight. But he forgot his concern as he got to work.

Benny liked digging in the creek. He filled his bucket quickly, then began rinsing and sorting.

"I have lots of pretty rocks," he said to Jonathan. "But I don't know if anything is good."

Jonathan pulled a dark red stone from his shirt pocket. "I brought this old garnet to test with." He picked a pinkish stone from Benny's tray and rubbed it across the surface of the garnet.

"It didn't leave a mark," Benny said, watching closely.

Henry came over. "That's because the

garnet is harder than your stone, Benny. If you had found a ruby, it would have scratched the garnet."

"Henry's right," said Jonathan. "Gemstones are rated by hardness. A diamond is at the top of the scale since it is the hardest stone. The softest stone, talc, is at the bottom. Any stone scratches talc, but only another diamond can scratch a diamond."

"I read about that in the museum," Henry said. "Rubies and sapphires are just below diamonds on the hardness scale."

Benny was confused with all this discussion. "So what did I find?"

"Rose quartz," Jonathan said.

"That's a nice stone," Jessie told her little brother.

"Yeah, but we can't win the contest with it," Benny said, disappointed.

Jonathan scooped ore into his tray. "I was hoping to find something really unusual for my fiancée's ring. So far, I haven't had much luck, either."

Henry straightened up from digging. He thought he saw a shadow among the pine trees along the trail. Something flashed in the bright sun. A mirror? Who would be shining a mirror up there? Had Cecil come back?

Just then Benny cried, "Hey! I found something really good this time!"

Jonathan examined Benny's find. "Hmmm. This does look interesting."

The others stopped working and came over.

"What is it?" asked Violet. "Let's check the hardness."

Jonathan rubbed Benny's stone against his garnet. "Oops!"

He dropped Benny's stone, which fell with a plop into the creek.

"My rock!" Benny fished around in the water.

Everyone searched along the bottom, but Benny's stone was gone.

"I'm sorry, Benny," Jonathan apologized. "My fingers were wet. Your rock just slipped."

"It's okay," said Benny.

The kids all went back to digging and

rinsing. Soon their collection bucket had several small sapphires and pinkish garnets Jonathan said were rhodolite garnets.

"I think it's time to break for lunch," Jonathan said. He called to Sybil, "Time to eat!"

Sybil waded over. "I hope you kids had better luck than I did." She rattled her plastic container. "I found a few sapphires, but nothing bigger than a grain of rice."

"We found sapphires, too," said Jessie.

Just as Jessie stooped to pick up their collection bucket, Sybil's foot flew out and knocked it over.

"Our rocks!" Benny plunged his hands to the creek bottom, but the stones were swirling downstream.

"I'm so sorry!" Sybil said. "I just lost my balance. I can't believe how clumsy I am."

Jessie couldn't believe it, either. Sybil hadn't lost her balance. She had kicked the bucket over. It was definitely no accident.

Sybil and Jonathan walked ahead of the Alden children on the way to the restaurant.

"Something funny is going on here,"

Jessie said. "Sybil deliberately made us lose our stones. But why?"

"Maybe she was jealous because she didn't find anything good," Benny said. Then he had a thought. "What about Jonathan? Do you think he dropped my rock accidently on purpose, too?"

"I don't know what is going on around here," said Henry. "But something is weird. While we were digging, I saw somebody in the trees." He described the flashing in the sun.

"It could have been a mirror," said Violet. "But it may have been binoculars. Or a camera. Those are both shiny."

Jessie nodded. "If the flash was a mirror, somebody could be signaling. If it was binoculars, somebody was spying on us. And if it was a camera, somebody took our picture."

"No matter what it was," Henry concluded, "someone is up to no good."

That night after dinner, the kids got together in Benny and Henry's cabin to discuss the mystery.

Jessie, who was very organized, wrote down the strange things that had happened.

"One," she said, "somebody took my backpack and returned it to our cabin. Two, Sybil and Jonathan both made us lose our stones in the creek. Three, somebody may have been taking our picture or spying on us."

"Why?" asked Violet. "None of this makes any sense."

Henry went to the window. "Do you hear that?"

Over the chirping of crickets came a faint, steady chipping noise.

"It sounds like digging," said Benny.

They all stared out into the darkness.

"There!" Henry pointed down the hill.

A figure in white flitted around the waterwheel.

"Is somebody down there digging?" Benny asked.

"Who would be working on the flume line after dark?" Jessie wondered aloud.

Violet answered. "Somebody who doesn't want to be seen during the day."

CHAPTER 6

Jessie's Treasure

"Let's go look at the place where we saw that person last night," Benny said the next morning.

"Before breakfast?" Violet asked, teasing her brother. "I thought you'd be starving, like always."

"A new mystery is more important," Benny declared.

"It'll only take a few minutes," Henry said, leading the way down the trail.

At the flume, Jessie stopped and looked

down. "Somebody was digging, all right. See the shovel marks?"

Benny nudged the pile of loose dirt with the toe of his sneaker.

"Isn't this where Donald Hodge dumped his buckets the other day?" he asked.

"You're right!" Violet said. "He threw his ore away and complained he couldn't find anything."

"But that doesn't answer who would come back after dark," Henry said. "What was that person looking for?"

"This is a tougher case than I thought," Benny said. "We definitely can't solve it before breakfast."

Jessie laughed. "Is that a hint? Okay, let's go eat!"

After breakfast, the Aldens went to the entry booth. Grandfather bought everyone a large bucket of native stone.

Donald, Jonathan, and Sybil each ordered one as well. With only a few more days in the contest, everyone was eager to pan as many buckets as possible.

"I want to see my buckets being filled,"

Donald said to the woman at the entry booth.

"I'm sorry, sir," she said, hefting his buckets onto the wheelbarrow. "We're too busy for that today. Everyone is buying special buckets. A lot of them were filled last night."

"How do I know I'm not being cheated?" Donald said.

The woman looked worried. "I'll ask Mr. Knight to come down and you can talk to him."

"Never mind!" Donald pushed the wheelbarrow to the flume.

"I don't know why Donald is so suspicious," Sybil said as they all found places along the flume. "Cecil would never sell native-stone buckets that weren't filled with ore from his mine."

Henry wondered if Donald might not have reason to be suspicious. A lot of mysterious things had already happened at Ruby Hollow.

It was another hot day. The Aldens were glad the flume was shaded.

"These are good buckets," Jonathan remarked, as he worked next to Jessie. "I've found three rubies already."

The others were doing well, too. Everyone had stones in their plastic containers. Everyone except Jessie.

She rinsed the stubborn North Carolina ore thoroughly and carefully sorted through the rocks left behind, but couldn't find a single gemstone.

"I'll buy you another bucket," Grandfather told her.

"I still have a little more left in this one," she said, dumping the remaining ore into her tray.

As soon as she rinsed the tray in the rushing water, she saw a large rock in one corner. She picked it up and rubbed the dirt off with her fingers. Then she rinsed it again.

She held the huge, reddish, glossy rock up to the light.

Jonathan gasped. "Jessie! That's the biggest ruby I've ever seen!"

Jessie was so startled, she nearly dropped her stone. "You're kidding!"

Sybil left her place in the line and came over. She whistled at the size of Jessie's stone.

"Take it to the grading window," Sybil advised.

All the Aldens went with Jessie to the jewelry shop. No one else was at the grading window.

Jessie handed her rock to the man at the counter. "Jonathan said this is a ruby."

The man's eyes widened. "Young lady — not only is this an enormous ruby, it's a *star ruby!*"

"I found a 'Goldilocks'?" Jessie couldn't believe it.

The gem inspector was on the phone, dialing. "Mr. Knight needs to see this."

Cecil Knight came down from the main office immediately. He examined Jessie's ruby through a jeweler's loupe, a special lens that fit over one eye. After a moment, he looked up at the Aldens with a surprised grin on his face.

"Great day in the morning!" he exclaimed. "That's the biggest star ruby that's ever been found in this mine, at least since my family took it over."

"Is Jessie rich?" Benny wanted to know.

"Your sister could be very rich," Mr. Knight told him. "And famous as well."

Jessie blushed. "I don't want to be famous. And we have enough money."

"Some people believe that rubies bring the wearer health, wealth, and wisdom," Mr. Knight said to her. He winked at Grandfather. "But I think your granddaughter is already wise."

"She's the levelheaded one in the family," Grandfather agreed proudly.

Cecil Knight gave the stone back to Jessie. "If you should decide to make this into a ring — and it'll be a doozy! — wear it on your left hand. According to tradition, you won't have any enemies." Then he added, "If you decide to sell the stone, I'd love to have it in my museum."

Jessie wrapped the ruby in a piece of tissue that the man at the grading window gave her and put it in her plastic container. She slid the container carefully into the pocket of her backpack.

"Jessie, do you want me to keep your stone?" offered Grandfather. "It might be safer with me."

"I'd like to look at it more," she told him. "I won't let my pack out of my sight. I promise."

"Are you ready for lunch?" Grandfather asked the children.

Benny answered for all of them. "Yes!"

The dining room was nearly filled when the Aldens walked in. Many people stood up and cheered.

"Why is everyone clapping?" Violet asked Grandfather.

"I think it's because of Jessie's incredible find," he replied.

"How does it feel to discover a treasure?" Jonathan asked Jessie.

She sat down, embarrassed at all the attention. "It could have been any of us. The ruby just happened to be in my bucket — it was just luck."

"What are you going to do with it?" Sybil asked, passing the basket of Italian bread. Today was spaghetti day.

"I was thinking, suppose we sell the stone and buy books for that library that was struck by lightning," Jessie suggested. "But it's a family decision."

"That's a great idea!" Benny said. "Let's do it!"

The others agreed.

"Jessie's stone is bigger than yours," Sybil said to Donald. "*And* it's a star ruby. Unless somebody finds a bigger star ruby than Jessie's, she will win the contest."

"It isn't over until it's over," Donald said levelly.

After lunch, the kids went hiking again. When the afternoon shadows grew long, they headed back to the cabins.

Violet unlocked the door to her and Jessie's cabin. She immediately spotted a white envelope lying on the rug just inside the door.

"This has your name on it," she said, handing it to Jessie.

"It must be from Grandfather," Jessie said absently as she opened the envelope. Then she gasped.

"What is it?" Violet asked.

Wordlessly, Jessie showed the note to Violet.

WISE UP AND GO HOME — OR ELSE! read the crudely lettered message. It was unsigned.

"I guess Mr. Knight was wrong about the ruby protecting me," Jessie said in a worried voice. "I have made an enemy, after all."

Then another thought occurred to her.

What if the ruby I found has put us all *in danger?*

The girls told the boys about the note on their way to dinner.

"Let's not mention it to Grandfather," said Violet. "It would just worry him."

"We can solve this case ourselves," Henry said confidently. "We've figured out lots of mysteries before."

In the dining room, everyone was excitedly chatting about the contest. There was only one more day left.

"I sure wish that star ruby had been in my bucket," Sybil said wistfully. "I've been coming here for years and have never found one."

"Maybe you will tomorrow," said Benny. "Maybe we'll all find star rubies!"

The others laughed as they ate hamburgers and fries.

It was too dark and cool to linger outside after dinner. Even though the days were hot, late-summer nights in the mountains were chilly.

The Alden children went back to Violet and Jessie's cabin to discuss the mystery.

They passed Jessie's note around.

Henry noticed something about the paper.

"It's been ripped from a notebook," he said. "One of those little ones with three rings."

"Jonathan carries a notebook like that," Benny remembered. "He keeps his lists in it."

"That's right," Violet said, nodding. "But why would he send us a threatening note? He seems so nice."

"We can't rule out anyone as a suspect," said Jessie.

Just then there was a shout outside.

Henry ran to the door. "It's Mr. Knight!"

"Hey, everybody!" Cecil Knight called. "Come see this!"

Doors to all the cabins were flung open and guests streamed out onto the lawn. The Aldens ran out, too.

Strange globes of light hovered in the sky over the mountain. Everyone oohed and aahed.

"Those are the same lights we saw our first night here!" Benny exclaimed.

"They do look like flying saucers," Sybil remarked, tipping her head back.

"Now that I've seen them better," Jonathan muttered, "I think the lights are a trick of the atmosphere."

Seen them better? Violet wondered. When had Jonathan seen the lights before?

Just as suddenly as the lights appeared,

they vanished behind the crest of the mountain. The show over, the guests filed back inside their cabins.

When Jessie walked into their cabin, she sensed something was wrong.

Her backpack was on the floor where she had left it.

But the outer pocket was unzipped.

She dug through it frantically.

"Violet!" she cried. "The ruby is *gone!*"

CHAPTER 7

The Robbery

Violet rushed over. "Oh, no! Are you sure?"

Jessie turned her backpack upside down. A comb, sunscreen, and a pack of mints tumbled out.

"I put the container in this pocket," she said. "That was the only thing I kept in it. It's empty! Someone stole the ruby!"

"We left our cabin door open to go look at the lights," Violet said with a sinking feeling. "Anyone could have walked in and taken it."

"I should have kept my backpack with me," Jessie said in dismay.

"We should have locked the door," Violet said. "Don't worry. We'll find the ruby." *I hope*, she added to herself.

The next morning, the girls hurried to the boys' cabin.

Grandfather was there, filling a basket with laundry. He and the boys stopped gathering towels to listen as Jessie related the story of the robbery.

Grandfather frowned with concern.

"This is very serious," he said. "We must go to Mr. Knight right away. There is a thief here, and we need to call the authorities."

The children glanced at one another.

"Grandfather," Henry said. "You know we're pretty good at solving mysteries."

James Alden nodded. "Yes, you are. But a valuable gemstone is missing."

"The police don't know any of the people here," Jessie pointed out. "But we do. The robbery may be connected to the contest. It'll be over tomorrow evening. Please let us try to find the ruby first."

Grandfather considered a moment. "All right," he agreed. "I'll give you until tomorrow evening. But if you can't find the stone by then, we'll go to Mr. Knight."

Jessie and Violet hurried back to their cabin to gather their own laundry. Then the children went with Grandfather to the Laundromat behind the main building.

The Laundromat was made of cement blocks. A bench with extra baskets stored beneath was placed below the single window.

Inside, the Laundromat was empty. Washers and dryers filled two walls of the small, dim building. Grandfather loaded one of the washers and plugged the slots with quarters. Then they all walked over to the dining room.

Donald and Sybil were already at their table, sipping juice.

As soon as the Aldens sat down, a waitress brought over platters of hotcakes and bacon.

"Did Jonathan eat already?" Sybil asked.

"No, ma'am," the waitress replied. "I haven't seen him this morning."

Donald raised an eyebrow. "He never misses a meal."

Violet glanced at the empty chair. *Where is Jonathan?* she wondered. Did he have anything to do with the missing ruby?

When breakfast was over, Grandfather returned to the Laundromat. The Alden children found a quiet spot in the picnic area to discuss the case.

"It's not like Jonathan to skip breakfast," Violet commented.

"Yeah," agreed Benny. "He always writes down whatever he eats."

"Maybe he's gone. Maybe he left Ruby Hollow because he has what he came for," Henry said. "He wanted a special stone for his fiancée's ring. A star ruby is very special."

"I just can't believe Jonathan took the ruby," said Jessie. "He's so nice."

"Everybody is a suspect," Violet reminded her. "Sybil Finley really wants a star ruby, too."

Henry nodded. "That's right. She told us the first day that a star ruby is the only stone she doesn't have in her collection."

"Plus her cabin is next to ours," Jessie said, ticking each item off on her fingers. "And she seemed interested in Violet's backpack at lunch the day Violet found her ruby. Sybil saw Violet put her ruby in her backpack in line at the grading window."

"She could have taken Jessie's backpack, thinking it was Violet's," said Benny. "And she knocked our bucket over at the creek."

"That's a pretty strong case against Sybil, but don't forget Donald Hodge," said Henry.

"He said he's going to win the contest," Benny put in. "He found a great big ruby. But Jessie's is bigger."

"Donald wants to win so he can buy a sports car," Henry said. "If he got rid of Jessie's ruby, he wouldn't have any competition. He'd still win the contest with his Papa Bear ruby."

"Any of them could have taken the star

ruby," Jessie concluded with a sigh. "We'll have to watch them all."

"We only have today and part of tomorrow," Violet said. "I hope we can solve this mystery in time."

A rustling sound made the children look up. A bent-over figure at another table was busy shuffling papers.

"There's Jonathan!" said Benny. "He didn't leave after all!"

"Let's go say hi," said Jessie. "And ask him why he wasn't at breakfast."

The Aldens approached his table. The surface was covered with loose pages from the black notebook Jonathan carried everywhere.

"Hi, Jonathan!" Benny greeted.

"Oh, hi, kids." Jonathan barely glanced at them. He ran his fingers through his sandy hair, clearly distracted.

"We missed you at breakfast this morning," said Jessie.

"It was good, too," Benny said. "Hotcakes and bacon!"

"I'm sure it was good, but I wasn't very hungry." Jonathan hastily pushed his papers into a messy pile, as if he didn't want anyone to see them.

"I bet you're hungry now," Violet said. "We're going to have a picnic for lunch. Would you like to come with us?"

"No, thanks." Jonathan stuffed the papers into a folder, then left.

Jessie watched him hurry up the trail. "That was weird. Usually he's very friendly. I wonder what's up?"

"Maybe he feels guilty," Henry guessed. "Because he stole our ruby."

"But why would he still be here?" asked Violet. "If he stole the ruby, you'd think he would be long gone."

"We should check on Sybil and Donald, too," Jessie said. "They're probably down at the flume."

Sybil was in her usual place on the flume line, but there was no sign of Donald. The flume was crowded with people hoping to find a prizewinning stone before the contest closed.

Cecil Knight was helping at the entry booth.

"Going to try your luck today?" he asked the kids, then laughed. "If I found a gem like yours, Jessie, I'd take it easy!"

They didn't want anyone besides Grandfather to know the ruby was missing, so Jessie hastily changed the subject.

"Mr. Knight, we'd like to have a picnic," she said. "May we pack a lunch?"

"Sure," he said. "Just ask the waitress to fix you something."

The tables in the dining room were set for lunch, but no one was around. One of the big windows overlooked the parking lot.

Henry looked out and saw a man in sunglasses and a large hat get into a car.

"Isn't that Donald?" he said. "I wonder where he's going."

The waitress appeared, carrying a tray of ketchup bottles.

"Maybe he's going into town for lunch," the waitress said. "Or shopping."

"Are there many stores in town?" Benny asked.

"Several nice shops," the waitress answered. "Even a gem shop. So if you don't find what you want here, you can go into town and buy it."

"Has Mr. Hodge gone into town before?" Henry asked.

"I don't know," said the waitress. Then she added, "He may have gone in to shop for binoculars."

"Why do you say that?" Jessie asked.

"I found him in Mr. Knight's office the other day," the waitress said. "He said he was borrowing Mr. Knight's binoculars."

"That's interesting," Henry said. He was eager to go to lunch so he and the other children could go back to talking about the mystery. "We were wondering if we could take a picnic lunch."

"Of course," the waitress said. "Be back in a jiffy."

Soon the children were on their way back to the picnic area. Violet carried the cloth-covered basket while Henry carried the thermos of lemonade.

Running ahead to choose the best table,

Benny spied a sheet of paper on the path. He picked it up.

"This looks like it came from Jonathan's notebook," he said, handing the paper to Jessie.

"It's a list," said Jessie. " 'Sapphire, garnet, ruby, emerald, blue calcite.' Those are all crossed off. Only one item hasn't been crossed off."

"Let me guess," said Henry. "Star ruby."

"Right." Jessie held out the paper. "Look what's written next to it."

Carrie's ring.

"Jonathan definitely wrote this," said Jessie. "He's after a star ruby for his fiancée's ring. Seems like he's our number one suspect."

Henry thought of something. "Jessie, do you have that other note? Let's compare the handwriting."

But the handwriting on the warning note did not match the handwriting on the list.

"If Jonathan took the ruby," Benny asked, "who sent the note?"

"Maybe the person who wants us to leave

is not the same person who stole the ruby," Jessie concluded. "I still think Jonathan took the ruby."

Henry shook his head. "We don't have enough evidence to accuse Jonathan. This is a serious crime. We need to be absolutely sure."

That evening, it was too chilly to go walking after dinner. Instead, the kids worked on a puzzle in Benny and Henry's cabin.

"Only one more day," Jessie sighed. "If we haven't found the ruby by tomorrow evening, we have to tell Mr. Knight."

"We'll work even harder tomorrow," Violet said, fitting a piece into the puzzle border.

Henry looked up. "Do you hear that?"

"Yeah," Benny said. "Sounds like digging."

"Grab a jacket," Henry told the others. "We're going down to the flume."

The moon was bright overhead, lighting the trail to the flume. As the kids rounded the empty entry booth, they saw a figure wearing a white shirt.

The figure dropped a shovel and sprinted down the trail. Henry, who was in the lead, ran after the person. But when the figure disappeared into the woods, he gave up the chase.

"Did you see who it was?" Violet asked him.

"No," he replied, disappointed. "Whoever it was just vanished into thin air!"

CHAPTER 8

Buried Treasure

The chalkboard outside the dining room announced possible storms later that day.

Violet read the breakfast menu printed below the weather forecast. " 'Contest Special — Native-Stone Buckets and Star Ruby Muffins.' "

"We're having *dirt* for breakfast?" Benny said. He liked playing in the dirt, but he didn't want to eat any!

"Today is the last day of the contest," said

Grandfather. "Everybody will need a hearty meal before going to work."

The Aldens sat down at their table, greeting Sybil, Jonathan, and Donald.

Henry noticed that Donald and Sybil looked tired, as if neither had slept very well.

Maybe, he thought, one of them was up late, digging around the flume.

The waitress brought glasses of ruby-red grapefruit juice.

"How would you like your Miner's eggs?" she asked, pen poised over her pad.

Jonathan grinned. "How about Hard as a Rock?"

Violet giggled. Jonathan was always telling jokes! How could he be the thief?

After eating eggs, Star Ruby cranberry muffins, and cups of Native-Stone Bucket granola, the Aldens walked down to the flume.

Cecil Knight was busy at the booth, collecting entry fees and handing out pre-spaded buckets.

Donald was in line in front of the Aldens.

"I know what you do," he accused Mr. Knight. "You salt those so-called native-stone buckets! You put a star ruby in some kid's bucket, just to make me lose the contest!"

Donald's voice was loud. Whispers rippled through the line.

"That is not true," Cecil said reasonably. "I run an honest operation here, just as my parents did when they bought the mine fifty years ago."

"It seems awfully funny that that kid — " Donald jerked his thumb toward Jessie — "found a star ruby when no one else has found one since 1988."

"Everyone has an equal chance," Cecil said. "That's the fun of panning. Now, what will you have today, Mr. Hodge?"

Donald ordered seven native-stone buckets.

While Grandfather was buying a "rainbow" bucket for each of them, Henry watched Donald walk down to the flume.

How did Donald know the last star ruby found at the Ruby Hollow Mine was in 1988? he wondered.

"What's supposed to be in a rainbow bucket?" Jessie asked Jonathan as they picked up trays.

"Rubies, sapphires, emeralds, pink sapphires," Jonathan replied. "Stones the colors of the rainbow."

After two hours of panning, Henry found an emerald and Benny found a blue sapphire. Jessie's bucket yielded a pink sapphire. Violet was delighted to find a purple stone called an amethyst. Purple was her favorite color.

When their buckets were empty, the kids cleaned up at the pump.

"I have something to check out," Henry said in a low voice. "Let's go back to the main building."

"You know who's missing here?" Jessie observed as they put their trays back on the stack. "Sybil."

"You're right," said Benny. "She's always

down here working. I wonder where she is today."

Away from the flume line, Henry told the others about Donald's remark. "How did he know when the last star ruby was found here?" he said.

"Maybe he read about it — there are a lot of newspaper articles on the wall in the lobby," said Violet.

"There's Sybil," Benny said.

The older woman carried a Ruby Hollow laundry basket up the path to the Laundromat. A white shirt dropped off the pile, but Sybil hurried on, unaware.

Benny ran ahead and picked up the shirt. He started to call out to Sybil when he noticed something.

"What is it?" asked Jessie.

"Look," he said. "The sleeve is ripped. Do you think that piece of cloth we found would fit?"

"Good thinking!" Henry praised. "Jessie, do you have that scrap with you?"

Jessie pulled the cloth from her pack,

where she kept the warning note and the list from Jonathan's notebook. She placed the scrap over the rectangular-shaped tear in the shirt.

Violet squinted. "It doesn't quite fit. One side is too long."

Henry held the shirt up to the light. "The material doesn't match." He pointed to the faint stain on the scrap. "This shirt doesn't have any stains."

"So it's not a good clue," said Benny, disappointed.

"We could be on the right track," Henry said. "Sybil had a lot of white clothes in her basket."

"I wonder if there's a stained shirt in her laundry," Violet mused.

"We have to watch her," said Jessie. "And Donald and Jonathan. It's hard to watch all these people when they are in different places. I wish they would stay in one spot!"

"That may not happen till this evening," said Violet with a sigh. "When the contest is judged."

"We *have* to find the ruby before then," Benny stated.

During lunch, Cecil Knight announced that the flume would close at five that evening, so the contest could be judged at six.

Jessie was glad. With only a few hours to find a special stone, everyone spent the afternoon on the flume, including Sybil, Donald, and Jonathan.

To make the time pass, Jonathan started telling jokes.

"Where do cows go on vacation?" he said to Benny.

"I don't know," Benny said. "Where?"

"Moo York!"

"Bad!" Violet declared, giggling. "But funny!"

"Where does a two-thousand-pound elephant sleep?" Jonathan asked.

"I give up," Benny said. "Where?"

"Anywhere he wants!" said Jonathan.

"I have one!" Benny said. "Where do rocks sleep?" Without waiting for anyone to guess, he blurted, "In a bed of rocks!"

"That's pretty good!" said Sybil, chuckling.

Jessie thought about Benny's joke. *In a bed of rocks.* It reminded her of something. But what? The thought nagged at her while she rinsed and sorted her stones.

After a while, she heard someone say, "Uh-oh."

Donald Hodge pointed to the sky.

Black clouds had formed over the mountain. Thunder grumbled. The weather forecast had been right on target.

Cecil Knight ordered, "Get inside! Get away from the water until the storm is over!"

"These mountain thunderstorms sure come up quickly," Grandfather said, herding the children up the trail to the main building.

Hot chocolate and oatmeal cookies were served in the dining room while the storm rumbled around them. Lightning flickered above the trees and sheets of rain dashed against the windows.

"I hope that library in town doesn't get hit again," said Violet.

"This isn't a very bad storm," Cecil Knight reassured her. "The sun will be shining again before we know it."

Within minutes the sky lightened and the downpour slowed to a drizzle.

While people chatted over hot chocolate and cookies, Jessie went over to the windows. Rainwater formed a small river across the parking lot.

The runoff was pretty strong, Jessie noticed. The muddy water reminded her of something.

"Let's go down to the flume," she whispered to the others.

They slipped out of the dining room unnoticed and ran down the trail. Water dripped from the roof of the flume and the grass was slick with rain.

"Okay, why are we here?" Henry asked Jessie.

She handed out spades. "I think I know what the mystery digger was doing."

"What?" asked Violet.

"Our mystery digger wasn't trying to *find* something," Jessie answered. "He — or she — was trying to *hide* something."

She pushed her spade into the wet dirt of the "dump" pile where people emptied ore from their trays.

Violet, Henry, and Benny began digging, too.

They didn't have to dig long. The heavy rains had washed away most of the pile.

"I hit something!" Benny exclaimed. "My spade scraped over something hard."

Jessie knelt down and pulled the object out of the hole, revealing a mud-caked square box.

"What is that?" asked Henry.

Jessie pried open the lid of the container. Inside, wrapped in damp tissue, was a single large stone.

"It's the star ruby," she proclaimed.

CHAPTER 9

"This Is My Final Warning!"

The others crowded around Jessie.

"It *is* the star ruby!" Benny breathed. "How did you know it was in the dirt pile?"

"Your joke about rocks sleeping in a bed of rocks gave me the idea to look here," Jessie said to him. "And when I saw that rain river in the parking lot, I figured a lot of the dirt would be washed away."

Henry nodded. "Good thinking. The second time we saw the person, he could have been burying the stone. But what about the first time? You hadn't even found the star ruby yet, Jessie."

"Maybe the thief hid something else there first," Violet suggested. "We don't know what else he may have stolen."

"Or she. We still don't know who took the ruby," Benny reminded them. "I wish we had more clues."

"All we have is the warning note, Jonathan's list, and a scrap of white cloth. Not much to go on," Jessie admitted. "At least we have the ruby back. Let's go tell Grandfather."

"And let's check to see if there's an article about when the last star ruby was found at this mine," Henry added.

Once more, the kids hurried up the hill to the main building.

Grandfather was in his room, reading the newspaper. He was glad the children had found the ruby, but was still concerned there was a thief in the resort.

"We still have to inform Mr. Knight," he said firmly.

"The contest is being judged tonight,"

Henry said. "I'm pretty sure we'll know who the thief is by then."

"All right," James Alden relented. "But as soon as the contest is over, we're going to Mr. Knight."

In the lobby, Violet signaled the others to come over to the wall of clippings and photographs.

"I don't see anything here about a star ruby being found in 1988," she said. "Maybe Donald Hodge read it in a guidebook or something."

Henry indicated his watch. "We have about forty-five minutes to find out who stole the ruby. The contest will be judged at six. What can we do to speed up our investigation?"

Violet had been thinking. "So far, we've been watching our suspects to see if we can figure out which one took the ruby. What if we did something to make the thief watch *us* instead?"

"I don't understand," said Benny.

"I do!" Jessie said. "Violet, that's a great idea! Make the thief show himself — or

herself. How can we get his attention?"

Henry snapped his fingers. "We let each of them know we have the ruby! The real thief will take notice!"

They found Jonathan first. He was sitting on the porch, his feet up on the rail, enjoying a frosty glass of lemonade.

"Hey, kids," he greeted. "I found a really nice sapphire today. It might be worth honorable mention in the contest."

"When the contest is over, we've decided to sell the ruby to Mr. Knight's museum," Jessie said casually. "Then we can buy books for that library."

Jonathan straightened up, setting his drink on the arm of his chair with a thump. "You're selling the star ruby to Cecil Knight? Do you know how much it's worth?"

"Maybe you can buy it from Mr. Knight and put it in your girlfriend's ring," Benny said.

"I couldn't afford to buy a star ruby of that size," Jonathan said. "I'm surprised Cecil can. It must be worth thousands!"

Henry blinked. "Thousands? Boy, we'll be able to buy a lot of books for that library."

"Good luck at the contest," Jonathan said, finishing his drink.

"What do you mean?" said Violet. "Isn't Jessie's ruby the biggest?"

Jonathan rocked back in his chair once more. "You never know," he said mysteriously. "You just never know."

The kids left to find Sybil and Donald.

"Did you see how Jonathan acted when Jessie mentioned we were selling the ruby?" Violet said. "He was surprised."

"Maybe he was surprised because we're selling it to Mr. Knight," Jessie said.

"Or maybe he was surprised because we *had* the ruby," said Henry.

At that moment, Cecil Knight came down the path. He grinned when he saw the kids.

"I hope you'll consider selling that beautiful stone to me," he said. "I'd be proud to have it in my museum."

"Well . . ." Jessie hesitated.

But Mr. Knight was distracted by one of his employees. "Be sure to lock the creek shed. You forgot the other night," he told the man.

"I'm sorry, kids," he said, turning back to the Aldens. "I need to go set up for the contest."

When he was gone again, Violet said, "We might have another suspect. Cecil Knight."

"Cecil?" said Benny. "Why him?"

"He wants the ruby for his museum," said Violet. "And he was the one who called everyone out to see the Brown Mountain Lights. Maybe he sent someone into our cabin to take the ruby."

Henry nodded. "Good point. We'll watch him, too."

They met Sybil on the path, coming from her cabin.

"Almost contest time!" she sang. "Are you excited?"

"We were just going to get the ruby from our cabin," Violet said.

Sybil was shocked. "You shouldn't leave that valuable stone in your cabin! The locks on those doors aren't very secure."

"It seems pretty safe here," Jessie said innocently. "Well, we'd better get ready for dinner. See you later!"

The Aldens walked down the path until Sybil was out of sight.

"She was surprised, too," Benny observed.

"Sybil sounded like she was worried about us leaving the stone in our cabin," said Violet. "But she could have been acting."

"I'm not leaving the ruby in our cabin again unless we're there," said Jessie, patting her backpack.

"So far all of our suspects are still suspects," Henry said. "But we have one more to track down — Donald Hodge."

Donald wasn't on the porch, or in the lobby, or at the gem museum. They didn't find him down by the stream, or around the picnic area.

"Maybe he's in his cabin," said Benny. It was almost suppertime and he was getting hungry.

"We don't know if he's staying in a cabin or in the main building like Grandfather," said Violet. "There's one place we haven't checked — the Laundromat."

No one was in there.

A load of freshly dried laundry was folded in a basket by the washing machine. Another load of clothes was piled sloppily on the dryer.

Benny went over to the basket on the floor. He recognized the white shirt lying on top.

"This looks like the shirt that fell out of Sybil's basket yesterday," he said. "She sure does a lot of laundry."

Jessie lifted a towel from the wrinkled pile on top of the dryer. "The clothes in that basket are hers, but I doubt these are. Sybil's too neat to leave such a mess."

"We might as well go — " Henry began.

As Jessie turned to leave, she accidentally brushed the pile of laundry onto the floor. "Oh, no," she said, hastily picking up the clothes. "I'm getting somebody's stuff dirty." She paused. "Hey, look at this!"

The others hurried over.

Jessie held out a stained, white button-down shirt. The pocket was ripped in a rectangular shape.

"I wonder if the scrap we found will fit." She pulled the material from her pack.

This time the scrap fit perfectly.

"Now we know the person who ripped this shirt was down by the creek the other day," said Henry. "And this is a men's shirt!"

"That doesn't mean anything," Violet said. "Sybil wears men's shirts sometimes."

Benny noticed something on the floor in the crack between the washer and dryer. He reached his small arm into the space and pulled out a tiny black velvet sack closed with a drawstring cord.

"Look what I found," he said.

Henry took the little sack and pulled the drawstring. An enormous ruby rolled into his palm.

He whistled. "This is Donald's Papa Bear

ruby! Remember? He showed it to us at lunch the first day."

"I bet it fell out of his pocket when he leaned over to take his clothes out of the dryer," Violet figured. "It's kind of dark in here. Donald might not have seen a black bag on the floor."

Henry was studying the gemstone intently. "He wouldn't let Jonathan touch this, remember? It was almost as if he didn't want anyone to see it closely." He looked at Jessie. "Let me have our star ruby."

Jessie gave him the plastic container. "What is it?"

"I want to try something," said Henry.

He held the star ruby in his right hand and Donald Hodge's ruby in his left. Then he scratched the star ruby across Donald's stone.

Violet gasped. "How did — ?"

At that moment the door slammed shut.

"I told you to go home!" growled a voice outside. "This is my final warning!"

Footsteps moved away from the door and down the path.

Benny ran over and tugged on the handle. "It won't open!" he cried.

Jessie twisted the handle. "It's locked or blocked or something!"

Henry glanced at his watch. "The contest closes in fifteen minutes! If we don't enter our star ruby, we'll lose!"

CHAPTER 10

A Thief Among Us

"We have to get out!" said Violet.

Henry stared at the small window. "There's a bench on the other side of that window. But only Benny will fit."

"It's the only way out," said Benny. "I'll go."

Henry linked his fingers together. "Step in my hands. I'll boost you on the count of three. One, two, *three!*"

Once he was level with the sill, Benny unlatched and opened the window. Then he crawled out.

Jessie let out her breath when she heard her brother drop safely onto the bench on the other side.

The door burst open and Benny ran inside.

"It wasn't even locked," he exclaimed, waving a stick. "This was jammed through the handle."

"We have to hurry!" Violet urged.

The children raced up the path to the main building. The dining room was packed with people.

"You enter the ruby," Henry told Jessie. "We'll find Grandfather."

Jessie spotted one of the resort's employees at the judging table. She ran up front, pulling the ruby case from her pack.

"I'm not too late, am I?" she gasped.

The man glanced at the clock over the stone fireplace. "Two minutes to spare, young lady."

After writing Jessie's name on his clipboard, he weighed the ruby and recorded it. Then he set the star ruby on a velvet pad next to a large ruby. Though there were many other rubies on the pad, the Aldens' was by far the largest. And it was the only star ruby.

Cecil Knight came over and consulted with his employee, then he stood on a chair and clapped loudly.

"Folks, may I have your attention?" he called. "I'm pleased to announce the winner of this year's Ruby Hollow gemstone contest. Without a doubt, the star ruby found by Jessie Alden takes the prize. Let's give her a hand."

Amid the applause, Jessie saw Donald Hodge get up and head for the doors.

Henry and Grandfather blocked his path.

"Let me through," Donald demanded.

"I'm sorry," said Grandfather. "But the children told me something about being locked in the Laundromat — "

"What's that got to do with me?" Donald said. "They were probably playing a game. You know how kids are."

"It wasn't a game," Violet insisted. "You put a stick through the handle so we couldn't get out."

"How do you know it was me?" asked Donald.

By now everyone in the dining room was listening. Jonathan and Sybil had joined the group by the door.

Cecil Knight left the judging table. "Is there a problem?" he asked.

"Yes," Henry answered. "Donald Hodge tried to keep us from entering our ruby in the contest."

Mr. Knight looked at him. "Let's go into my office."

"Jonathan and Sybil should come, too," said Jessie. Both of them agreed to go inside Mr. Knight's office and talk. Once everyone was inside, Mr. Knight closed the door and said, "Now, what is this all about?"

"Somebody took the ruby from my backpack," Jessie said.

"And we think the culprit is in this room," Violet added.

"Since when do children accuse adults of stealing?" Donald asked. "And how do we know the ruby was stolen if they have it back? She entered it in the contest!"

"I think we should listen to the kids," said Mr. Knight.

"We have evidence," said Jessie. She pulled the gem list from her pack.

Jonathan looked surprised. "That's mine."

"We found it on the ground in the picnic area," said Benny. "You crossed off everything but 'star ruby.' "

"You looked upset that day," Violet said.

Jonathan nodded sadly. "I had just gotten a letter from Carrie. She said I had been rock-hunting too long instead of visiting her. I was trying to write her a letter when you kids came along."

Sybil patted his shoulder. "I hope you called her."

"I did," Jonathan said. Then he looked alarmed. "You don't think I stole the star ruby? I'd never do that!"

Mr. Knight waved his hands. "Wait a minute. Tell us about the star ruby being stolen. And how you got it back."

"I kept it in my backpack," said Jessie. "The night we all went out to look at the Brown Mountain Lights, somebody went into our cabin and took the ruby."

Violet turned toward Jonathan. "You'd seen those lights before. You let it slip when you were talking to Sybil."

Jonathan blushed. "I'd heard about the lights, but I thought it was some story. I was walking in the woods when they appeared the night you Aldens arrived. I didn't say anything at breakfast the next morning because I was afraid I'd look silly."

"What do the lights have to do with stealing the ruby?" Donald persisted.

"Only that anyone had the chance that night to go in our cabin and take the ruby," Violet said. "We even thought someone who worked here could have taken it because Mr. Knight called everyone out to see the lights."

"These kids have wild imaginations," Donald said to Cecil Knight.

"Twice we heard someone digging in the

dump pile at the flume line after dark," Henry went on. "The person was wearing white. Once we chased the person, but whoever it was ran."

Now it was Sybil's turn to act sheepishly. "I'm afraid I'm the guilty party."

Mr. Knight stared at her. "What were you doing?"

"Donald threw away a lot of dirt. I thought there might be some good stones in his dump pile," Sybil answered. "But I was too embarrassed to let anyone see me, so I went out after dark. But I was only there once — and I didn't run away!"

"Who *did* run away?" Cecil Knight pursued.

"The person who stole the ruby," said Jessie. "We found the ruby buried in the dump pile."

Grandfather looked confused. "A valuable stone buried in a pile of dirt? That doesn't make sense."

"It's the perfect place," said Henry. "Who would think of looking in the dump pile?

But the thief got nervous and checked on it one night. When we went down there, the thief ran away."

Cecil Knight sat down at his desk. "Why would anyone be so dishonest?"

"Some people here are very interested in getting a star ruby for their collection," Grandfather put in, looking at Sybil.

"You don't think it was me?" Sybil asked, shocked. "Yes, I'd love a star ruby. But I wouldn't steal one! I felt bad enough kicking over the children's bucket the other day."

"So that *wasn't* on purpose," said Violet. "We thought you took Jessie's backpack at first, too," she added. "We found a scrap of white shirt material at the creek the day it was taken. And the day I found my Mama Bear ruby, you left the gem line in a hurry. At lunch later, you seemed very interested in my pack, which looks just like Jessie's."

"I can explain," said Sybil. "I had forgotten to take my medication and I remembered while I was in line. I went back to my cabin to take it. But I don't understand about your pack. I thought Jessie's pack was taken."

"It was," Jessie explained. "Mine looks just like Violet's."

"All this talk of rubies and backpacks!" Donald said scornfully. "What does this have to do with the robbery?"

"Because," said Henry, "the thief was interested in winning the contest."

"And who was it?" Cecil Knight demanded. "Who *is* the thief?"

Jessie produced the warning note. "The same person who wrote this. Donald Hodge."

Everyone sat stunned.

Then Donald's face turned a deep red. "How dare you accuse me! Anyone could have written that. What *real* proof do you have?"

"This." Henry pulled out the black velvet bag. "This is your Papa Bear ruby. We found it in the Laundromat. Jessie, let me have the star ruby again."

Jessie handed him the star ruby. Henry scratched the star ruby across Donald's ruby.

"Our ruby leaves a mark!" Benny said. "That means Donald's ruby isn't a ruby at all!"

Mr. Knight was amazed. "You were going to enter a fake ruby in the contest? That would never work."

"Donald must have known that," said Henry. "What I don't know is why he did it."

Donald shoved his hands in his pockets and glowered.

Benny stared at him. The way Donald was standing reminded him of something . . .

He went over to the wall and looked at the picture of the two boys standing by the waterwheel. The taller boy had his hands jammed in his pockets and was frowning into the camera.

"Look," Benny said, pointing to the photograph. "Donald looks just like the boy in this picture, the way he's standing."

Cecil Knight took the photograph off the wall. Then he looked carefully at Donald. "It *is* you!"

"Who?" asked Jonathan, puzzled.

"Mr. Knight's cousin," Benny said matter-of-factly. "He's the cousin who came to visit once."

"Cousin Don," Mr. Knight said. "I haven't seen you since you came with Uncle Josh and Aunt Cathy, forty years ago. So that's why you're always wearing sunglasses — you thought I'd recognize you. What are you doing here?"

"These kids think they're so smart," Donald sneered. "Why don't *they* tell you?"

"We can guess," said Henry. "You want Ruby Hollow."

"That's exactly it," Donald confessed angrily. "The mine should belong to me. My father said we got cheated. So I decided to come back and make trouble. I tried to make people think you run a dishonest operation."

"You took my backpack and returned it so we would complain," said Jessie. "But you ripped your shirt that day. We matched the scrap to the shirt you left in the Laundromat."

"You did things like complain about the buckets being salted," said Violet. "When Jessie found the star ruby, you took it. If everyone knew there was a thief here, they might leave. But we never reported the robbery."

"If you're such clever detectives," Donald said, "what else have you figured out?"

Henry had noticed something on the wall, too.

"We saw you spying on us the day we went creekin'," said Henry. "But you were really watching Mr. Knight, weren't you? You were in his office that day. Is that when you read about a star ruby being found here in 1988?"

"I was looking for Cecil's account books," Donald admitted. "I'd heard he was in debt."

"I was in debt a few years ago," Cecil Knight said. "But my business is doing better now. This winter I'm going to fix up the cabins." He shook his head. "I still don't understand why you had that fake ruby."

"I was going to enter it in the contest,

and when the judges called it a fake, I planned to tell everyone it came from one of the native-stone buckets you sold me," Donald explained.

"And then Jessie Alden found a star ruby that upset your plans," Sybil figured. "So you stole her ruby."

"I wanted to take away anything else I could — like this resort." Donald said.

"Never!" Cecil Knight stated. "Ruby Hollow Mine belongs to me and always will. I suggest you leave immediately. For Aunt Cathy's sake, I won't press charges."

Donald left the room in a huff.

"Thanks, kids," Mr. Knight said to the Aldens. "Don could have caused a lot of damage if it hadn't been for you."

"We're just glad everything turned out okay," said Jessie. "And if it's all right with Grandfather, we'd like to sell the ruby to you, for your museum."

Violet took her gem box over to Jonathan.

"I know this isn't a star ruby," she said. "It's not even a Papa Bear ruby. But I'd like to give it to you for Carrie. I think it would make a pretty ring."

Jonathan smiled at her. "Your ruby will make a very special ring. Thank you very much. I'll tell Carrie all about you Aldens."

Benny grinned. Another mystery solved!

Maybe, he thought, *we won't have to dig for our next case!*

GERTRUDE CHANDLER WARNER discovered when she was teaching that many readers who like an exciting story could find no books that were both easy and fun to read. She decided to try to meet this need, and her first book, *The Boxcar Children*, quickly proved she had succeeded.

Miss Warner drew on her own experiences to write the mystery. As a child she spent hours watching trains go by on the tracks opposite her family home. She often dreamed about what it would be like to set up housekeeping in a caboose or freight car — the situation the Alden children find themselves in.

When Miss Warner received requests for more adventures involving Henry, Jessie, Violet, and Benny Alden, she began additional stories. In each, she chose a special setting and introduced unusual or eccentric characters who liked the unpredictable.

While the mystery element is central to each of Miss Warner's books, she never thought of them as strictly juvenile mysteries. She liked to stress the Aldens' independence and resourcefulness and their solid New England devotion to using up and making do. The Aldens go about most of their adventures with as little adult supervision as possible — something else that delights young readers.

Miss Warner lived in Putnam, Connecticut, until her death in 1979. During her lifetime, she received hundreds of letters from girls and boys telling her how much they liked her books.